READING

RECOVERY

A Break-of-Day Book®

Ever since 1928, when Wanda Gág's classic *Millions of Cats* appeared, Coward, McCann & Geoghegan has been publishing books of high quality for young readers. Among them are the easy-to-read stories known as Break-of-Day books. This series appears under the colophon shown above—a rooster crowing in the sunrise—which is adapted from one of Wanda Gág's illustrations for *Tales from Grimm*.

Though the language used in Break-of-Day books is deliberately kept as clear and as simple as possible, the stories are not written in a controlled vocabulary. And while chosen to be within the grasp of readers in the primary grades, their content is far-ranging and varied enough to captivate children who have just begun crossing the momentous threshold into the world of books.

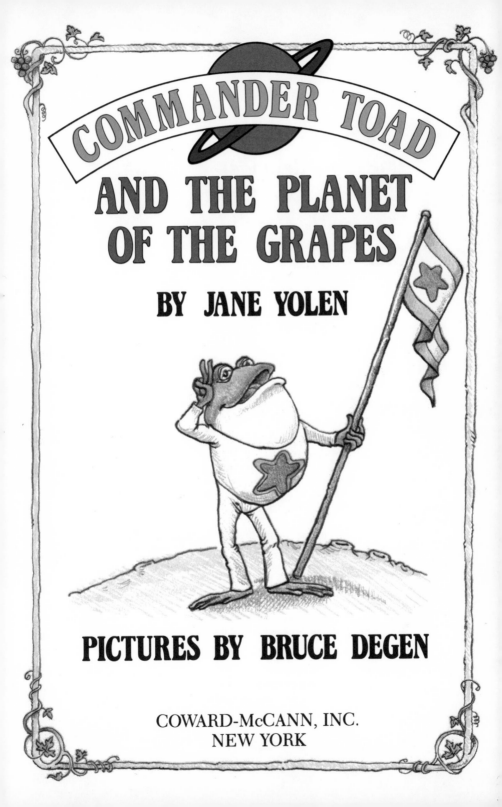

COMMANDER TOAD
AND THE PLANET
OF THE GRAPES

BY JANE YOLEN

PICTURES BY BRUCE DEGEN

COWARD-McCANN, INC.
NEW YORK

*For my Tad,
Alexander
(the Great)
—B.D.*

First paperback edition published 1982
Second printing
Library of Congress Cataloging in Publication Data
Yolen, Jane.
Commander Toad and the Planet of the Grapes.
Summary: In search of new worlds to explore, Commander
Toad and his crew land their space ship "Star Warts" on
the strange Planet of the Grapes.
[1. Toads—Fiction. 2. Science fiction] I. Degen,
Bruce. II. Title.
PZ7.Y78Cn [Fic] 81-3120
ISBN 0-698-30736-4 AACR2
ISBN 0-698-20540-5 pbk.

*For Mariette,
who has kept me laughing
since 10th grade
—J.Y.*

There are many ships
that fly
from star to star.
But only one
is long and green.
Only one
is flown by
Commander Toad.

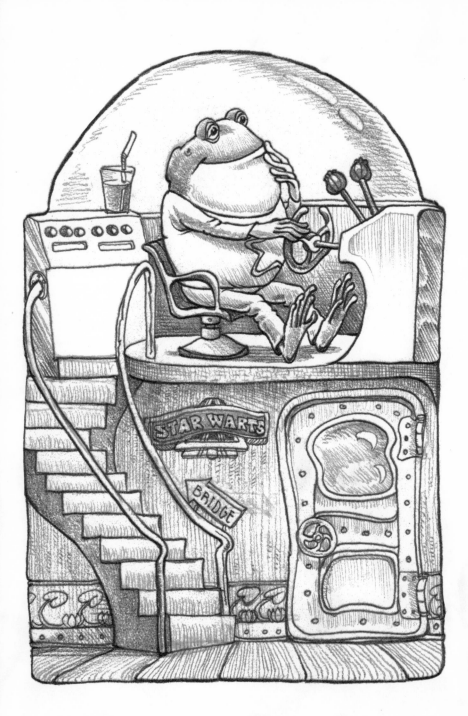

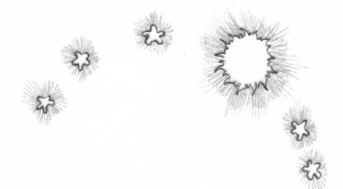

Brave and bright,
bright and brave,
Commander Toad
brings his ship
through deep hopper space.
That ship is called
the *Star Warts*.
Its mission:
to find new worlds,
to explore new planets,
to bring
a little bit of Earth
out to the alien stars.

Commander Toad
has a very fine crew.
Mr. Hop
is his copilot.
He thinks a lot.
His thoughts are
cool and deep
as winter ponds.

Lieutenant Lily
is in charge
of the engine room.
She knows every
rod and dial.
Young Jake Skyjumper
makes the maps
that show where they
are going
and where they have been.

And old Doc Peeper,
in his grass-green wig,
keeps them healthy
as they fly.

Many days
and many nights
go by in space.
Sometimes the crew
plays games
like chess
or checkers
or leapfrog-and-toad.

Sometimes
they sing songs.
"Hoppy birthday"
is one of their favorites.

And sometimes
they get very bored.
There is nothing to see
outside the ship
but deep, dark space
lit only by
the faraway stars.

At last a new planet
comes into sight.
"It is a fine place
for my tired crew,"
says brave and bright
Commander Toad.

The *Star Warts*
hangs over the planet
like a great green pickle.
Commander Toad
and Lieutenant Lily
sail down in
a little sky skimmer.
They will make sure
that nothing nasty
or mean
waits for the crew
on this brand-new world.

Commander Toad
leaps out of the skimmer
and laughs as he lands.
"A fine, quiet planet
for a picnic.
Come join me,
Lieutenant Lily."
Lily smiles.
Then she sneezes.
"Ah-chippity-choo.
There is something
on this calm world
I am allergic to,"
she says
and sneezes once again.

She wipes her nose
with a regulation
starfleet
nose-kerchief
and prepares to
leap from the skimmer.
But before she can move,
something begins to grow
under Commander Toad's feet.

First it is a bump.
Then it is a lump.
Then it is a bubble
that looks like
a giant grape.
"Wait a bit,"
warns Commander Toad.
"Things grow
too quickly
on this quiet world."

The bump-lump-grape
has become a bunch
of twenty or more
bumpy-lumpy things.
They move like
player-piano keys
under Commander Toad,
playing a silly
tickle song
on the bottoms of his
webbed feet.

"Ho-ho-ho,"
sings Commander Toad.
Hop-hop-hop
go his feet.

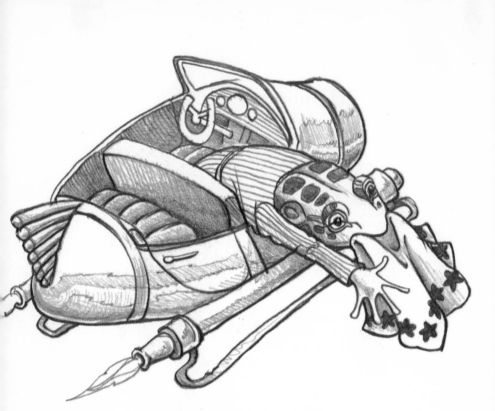

"Quick, Commander,"
Lieutenant Lily calls,
sneezing twice.
She leans over
the skimmer's side,
holding one hand
to her nose
and the other hand
out to Commander Toad.

"Stop hopping around
and hop in."
But it is too late.
As she watches,
one lump-bump
grows up and around
Commander Toad
and swallows him.

"Burp!" says the bubble grape.
"Oh, Commander,"
Lieutenant Lily cries.
She takes out her gun,
but she is afraid
to fire.
What if she hits
Commander Toad,
and what if he is not
a grape dinner
or a grape dessert,
but is only the guest
of a grape,
getting inside information
instead of getting eaten?

Lily puts her gu
She will go
up to the *Star*
She will ask the o ers
to help.
Mr. Hop will thin
Old Doc Peeper
will bring Band-Aids.
And young Jake Skyjumper
will stay on the ship.
"Don't go away,
Commander Toad,"
says Lieutenant Lily,
"Ah-chippity-choo."

"*Burp!*" says the grape.
Commander Toad
says nothing.
Lieutenant Lily
pushes the button
that sends the skimmer
up to the waiting ship.

On board again,
Lily tells them all
what has happened.

Mr. Hop
thinks for a moment,
his chin in his hand.
"Very interesting,"
says old Doc Peeper.
"I'll get my bag."

Then Doc Peeper
and Lieutenant Lily
and Mr. Hop
ride the skimmer down.
Only young Jake
is left aboard
to guide the great ship home
if anything bad happens
to the rest of the crew
on the calm but scary
Planet of the Grapes.

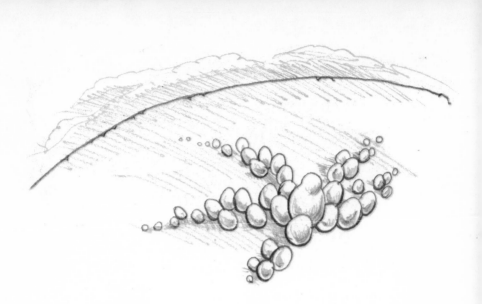

The skimmer hovers
above the planet,
where only a bunch
of great grapes
waits to greet them.
"One of those grapes
is Commander Toad,
brave and bright,
bright and brave,"
says Lieutenant Lily.
She sneezes.

"Which one?"
asks Mr. Hop.
"I do not know,"
says Lieutenant Lily.
"All grapes look alike to me."
"That one
might be the commander,"
says Mr. Hop.
"The one with the lump
where his hat
would be."
Mr. Hop calls down
to the lumpy grape.
"Don't worry, Commander.
We are here to help."

He turns to the others.
"I have been thinking:
As long as we
move very fast,
there will be no time
for a grape
to grab us."
He hops out.
"Wait!" cries Lily,
ending with a sneeze.
But it is too late.

No sooner
do Mr. Hop's feet
touch the ground
than a bunch of grapes
grows like blisters
all around him.
One grape,
bigger than the rest,
swallows Mr. Hop.
"Burp!" says the grape.
"Ah-chippity-choo,"
says Lieutenant Lily sadly.

"Very interesting,"
says old Doc Peeper.
He fixes his wig.
Then he takes
a great big needle
out of his bag.

38

"Before we save
Commander Toad
and Mr. Hop
from being graped,
I will give you a shot
to stop your sneezes
and your
chippity-choos.
It is hard to be brave
when your nose
is running
faster than your feet."

But while Doc Peeper
moves toward
Lieutenant Lily's
side of the skimmer,
an enormous bubble
is growing
underneath them.
It grows up
and around the skimmer,
quiet as air,
silent as sleep.

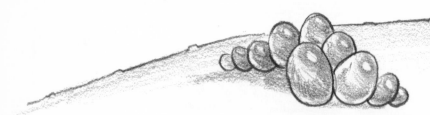

And before
Lieutenant Lily
can sneeze
or old Doc Peeper
can give her a shot,
the skimmer is caught
in the biggest lump
of them all.

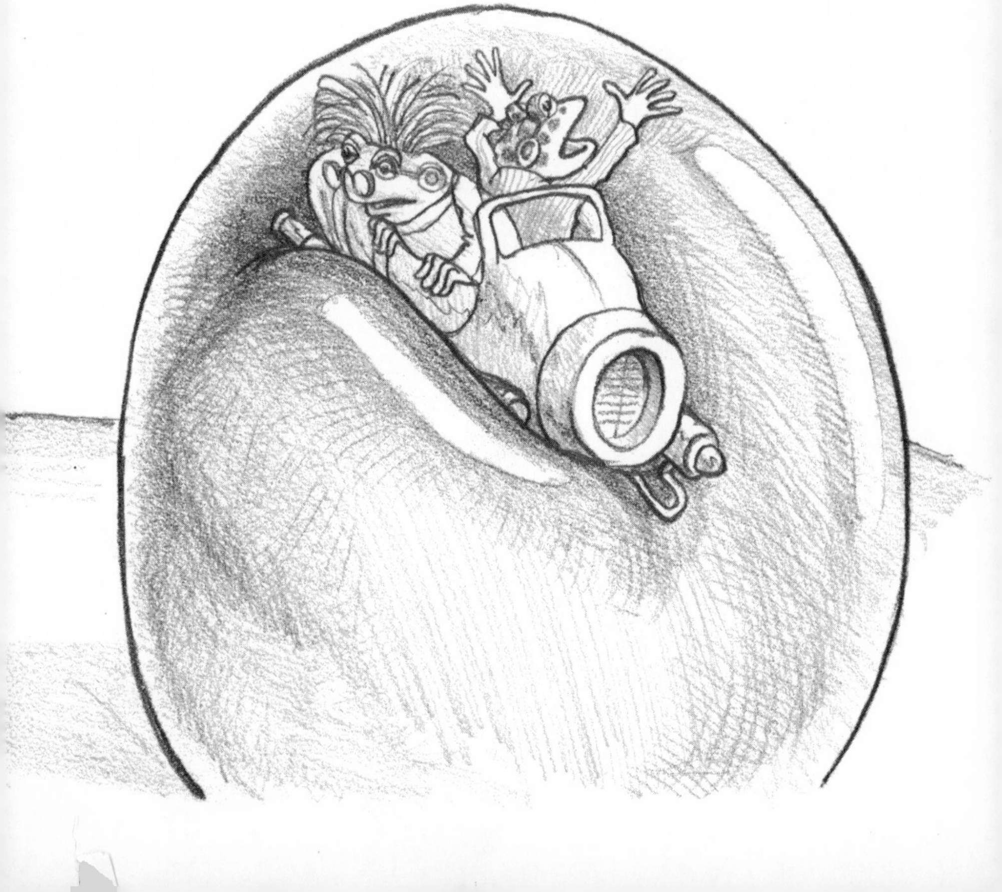

"This bump is so big,
it must be
Alexander the Grape,"
says Lieutenant Lily.
Doc Peeper groans.
It is dark
inside the grape,
and hot.
Doc Peeper
finds his flashlight.
He turns it on.
It makes things brighter
but it does not
make them clearer.

Suddenly
the sky skimmer
tips sideways,
and head over heels,
webbed feet over wig,
Lieutenant Lily
and Doc Peeper
are spilled out.

Lieutenant Lily
falls on her gun
and it jams.
Doc Peeper
falls on the handle
of his needle.

The needle
goes into the bubble—
Whoosh!—
and most of the medicine
is shot
into the bubble's side.
"Burp!" says
Alexander the Grape.

"*Ah-chippity-choo*,"
Lieutenant Lily replies.
Then far above them
is a sudden pinprick
of light.
Is it a window?
Is it a star?
Is it an opening
in the top of the grape?

Doc Peeper
gives Lily
the rest of the medicine
and then he gives her
a boost up.
She sticks her head
out of the hole
and looks around.

The opening grows wider.
Lieutenant Lily
crawls through.
Soon the grape
has opened like a flower.
Doc Peeper steps out.
"I do not get it,"
says Lieutenant Lily.
Doc Peeper says,
"I do."

He takes another needle
out of his black bag
and goes over to
the lump
with the hat.
No sooner does he give
the lump a shot
than the grape
peels itself
and out steps
Commander Toad.

51

"Have a grape day,"
says Commander Toad,
shaking Doc Peeper's hand.

Doc Peeper
gives a final shot
to the Mr. Hop lump.
When Mr. Hop
steps out,
he looks around.
"I am very grapeful
to be out of there,"
he says.

Commander Toad
leaps into the skimmer,
and behind him
come Mr. Hop,
Lieutenant Lily,
and old Doc Peeper.
The sky skimmer
lifts off.
"What was that
all about?"
asks Commander Toad.

Doc Peeper smiles.
"Just as Lily
is allergic
to the planet,
so this planet
is allergic
to us.
We gave it warts
and hives
and a bad
case of the grapes."

Lieutenant Lily
puts her hand to her nose.
"No more sneezes,"
she says.
"Your shot worked on me."

They look over
the side of the skimmer.
Far below, on the planet,
they can see
only one grape left.
It is wearing
a silly green wig.

"And it worked
on the planet, too,"
says Lieutenant Lily.
"Hummmmmm," says Mr. Hop.
"If the planet
is allergic to us,
it would not be
a good idea
to go back again.
Besides,
those grapes were
an awfully tight fit."

"And they liked
to *wine* a lot,"
says Commander Toad.
He slaps his leg
and laughs
at his own joke.
Old Doc Peeper
looks serious.
"There is something more,"
he says
as he puts the needle
into the bag.
"Anyone who sets foot
on that planet
seems to tell
very bad grape jokes."

"Bad?" says Commander Toad.
"I thought those jokes
were the grapest."

The sky skimmer
floats up
to the mother ship.
Jake Skyjumper
welcomes them aboard.
"I think we got away
just in time,"
says Commander Toad.
"There is *nothing* worse
than a *bad* grape joke."
"I do not get it,"
says Jake Skyjumper.
"Just be glad
that they did not get you,"
says Lieutenant Lily.

They tell him
all about it
as the ship takes off
into deep hopper space.
"Let's find some
new planets,"
says Commander Toad.

Then they leapfrog
across the galaxy
from star
to star
to star.